inside

Book 2

My New Normal™

Sara Michelle

SADDLEBACK℠
EDUCATIONAL PUBLISHING

$7.95

01-24-12

The Aftermath * Book 1

The Inside * Book 2

The Others * Book 3

EDUCATIONAL PUBLISHING
www.sdlback.com

Copyright ©2012 by Saddleback Educational Publishing
All rights reserved. No part of this book may be reproduced or transmitted in any form or by any means, electronic or mechanical, including photo-copying, recording, or by any information storage and retrieval system, without the written permission of the publisher.

ISBN-13: 978-1-61651-771-7
ISBN-10: 1-61651-771-9
eBook: 978-1-61247-351-2

Printed in Guangzhou, China
0911/CA21101549

16 15 14 13 12   1 2 3 4 5

Day 13

8:00 a.m.

I felt my brain slip out of its dream state. It was so comforting to finally wake up in an actual bed. I lay still, appreciating the moment before finally opening my eyes. They slowly opened, and I took in the scenery around me. The room was plain, but it was sturdy, safe, and I was finally able to claim something as my own.

Cecilia and I'd begun to consider the snow shelter as our temporary home. It was the first clean and suitable shelter we had since the earthquake almost two weeks ago. I shuddered at the pang of painful memories. I just didn't want to go there. Not yet. I don't think I could ever thank God enough for keeping me and the love of my life alive and, for the most part, healthy. It definitely wasn't the easiest weeks of my life, but we got through it together and with very little *physical* damage.

I'll never be able to get rid of the horrible memories of that day. The screaming. The boom. The flash of light. The gore. The pain. The complete blood-pumping horror. It was almost too much to bear. No matter how long I live, that day will never stop haunting me.

After traveling on foot for many days and nights, we now call the Denver Snow Shelter home ... at least for the time being. I can't explain how, in a time of such desperation, I was able to conveniently—brilliantly, if I say so—come up with the idea to come here. Luckily it was still intact. And I've been thankful for this space every moment of the last two days ... even if we've yet to figure out the many unexplained noises we continue to hear. We often wonder if it's the shelter or just the world itself trying to decide if it's truly finished with the horror it has unleashed.

I sat up and stretched, ready to continue working on our new normal—the new lives that we would build. The road to completing our goal was going to be rough. But with Cecilia—for Cecilia—I'd be able to accomplish anything. I was sure of it. I rolled myself out of bed and made my way over to the closet-sized bathroom.

I stared at my reflection and tried to figure out how a guy like me was still alive after this devastating earth alteration. My face looked scruffy since I hadn't shaved since the quake. My hair was getting too long, and the blond was fading more into a lighter brown, almost auburn. My arms were firm, and I had defined muscles in all the right places. My eyes, still a bright blue, never failed to be the biggest charmer for Cecilia. My girl.

I debated whether or not to hop in the shower or go see if she was awake.

Since we'd been here, I'd taken at least nine showers, taking advantage of the plentiful hot water. A very nice luxury considering the current state of affairs. Maybe it was too indulgent? I wasn't sure how long our luck would last.

It was so unbelievably hard to man-up and comfort Cecilia when I could barely stand the horrible conditions myself. All in all, I was just glad the initial struggle to survive was over. We were safe for the time being.

I decided against showering and instead went to see if Cecilia was awake. I walked out into the hallway and tiptoed up to her bedroom door. I knocked and waited a moment to see if she would answer. She didn't. I turned the doorknob and peeked inside. Her bed was perfectly made, and she was nowhere to be seen. I rolled my eyes. She'd always been the tidiest girl I'd ever known.

Day 13

9:00 a.m.

Just as I began to wonder where she could be, the smell of maple oatmeal and burned toast wafted down the hall. My stomach growled. I shut her door. Then I followed my nose into the large kitchen. I found her there stirring a pot of oatmeal. I came up behind her and wrapped my arms around her small waist. She yelped in surprise and turned to face me. Instead of her usual smile I got a scowl.

"Don't scare me like that while I'm cooking, Ryan," she scolded.

I removed my arms from around her waist and put my hands up in surrender.

"Sorry, Chef Boyardee," I replied sarcastically.

She rolled her eyes, turned her back to me, and continued stirring.

Geez! What was up with her this morning? She continued to finish cooking breakfast without saying a word. She soundlessly handed me a bowl of oatmeal and took her seat at the table. I followed her and took my own.

"What's wrong with you this morning?" I asked.

She took a spoonful of oatmeal and didn't meet my eye.

"Nothing," she replied quietly and continued eating.

This was totally suspicious. She was *never* pissed at me. Where was the attitude coming from?

When she was through eating, she stood up and grabbed my bowl. I wasn't exactly finished, but I decided it wouldn't be smart to protest right now.

I helped Cecilia clean up and grabbed her hand. She didn't pull away, but she held her hand limply in mine. I led her back to my room. I wanted to discuss the next step to moving on from this disaster. As much as we both avoided accepting it, the snow shelter wouldn't sustain us forever. I figured the supplies would last four to five weeks at the most. Who knows when the power would give? I wasn't sure about the water supply either. We had already used so much without thinking about conserving. It was scary to think about, but we had to be realistic. I opened my door. She took a seat on my bed.

"So what's today's agenda?" she asked quietly. Curiosity sparkled in her eyes, along with something else I couldn't put my finger on. I sat next to her and took her hand again.

"Eventually, we're going to have to start exploring the city. The snow shelter is a huge blessing. But realistically, it's not going to last us forever."

She rolled her eyes for what seemed like the hundredth time this morning. "I'm not a child. Or stupid. I know that. How long are we talking?"

Okay, honestly, I was getting a little irritated with her sore attitude. I hadn't done anything to her and didn't deserve to be treated so rudely. I just didn't understand girls. What was up? I took a deep breath and calmly replied, "I'd give us five weeks tops."

Cecilia looked down once again. "That soon?"

I felt so helpless looking at her. I felt all my irritation slip away. I hated not being able to fix things for her. This situation was way out of my control. I was willing to give up anything to go back to the way things were before we were enveloped in this inescapable hell.

I wrapped my arms around her. I tried my best to comfort and reassure her that somehow everything would be okay. But I really couldn't be convincing when I could barely convince myself. We were walking into an unknown world. A world without leadership. No government. No medicine. No transportation. No food except what we could grow ... or kill. It was going to be mass chaos.

This wasn't the first disaster the world had seen, but I was wondering if it would be the last. I'd no idea what we were getting into or how to handle what was to come. I'd had to man-up when my dad left my mom, but this was way out of my league. I was not prepared for our new normal.

"Cecilia, I can only tell you that we were chosen to survive for a reason. I have no idea what's going to happen now, but I'm going to do everything I can to turn this around for us."

Cecilia looked up at me and tried to read my eyes like she had so many times before. I tried to send signals of hope and belief, but it was weak. I knew she was able to read past me.

Surprisingly, she replied with a monotonous "okay," stood up, and left me sitting alone on the bed as she left the room.

Confusion and anger erupted throughout my body. Why was she being so pissy? I couldn't imagine anything I'd done that could've made her act the way she'd been acting. Throughout the whole time we've been dating, she's never acted like this without a legit reason.

Before I could decide whether to be worried or pissed, a sound distracted me. I could have sworn it was a knock, but Cecilia knew she didn't have to knock on my door.

"*Ryan*?!" Cecilia screamed.

I ran out into the hallway where Cecilia was—she was panicked. And white as a sheet.

"Was that you?" she whispered.

I shook my head. Once again we heard the faint sound of heavy knocking.

"Who could it be?" she asked.

Hope welled inside of me. "Maybe it's finally help!" I cried. "Maybe it was just *this* city that was totaled, and help is finally here!"

I grabbed Cecilia's hand and led her down the hallway up to the main entrance of the basement where the knocking continued.

"Ryan, why would it have taken this long for help?" she asked.

Her face looked uneasy and fear radiated from her eyes.

We climbed the stairs.

I smiled. "Cecilia, I have such a good feeling about this," I said as I approached the door. I was *so* wrong.

I turned the heavy deadbolts and opened the massive metal doors. I expected to see the police, a rescue squad, or maybe even a news crew. What I didn't expect was to see the man that was standing in front of me.

Day 13

10:00 a.m.

He was chubby and had a smirk on his face. His skin was deeply tan. He had wide eyes, and if it wasn't for his smirk, I would have thought he looked terrifying. His nose was too small for his face, and his lips were too big. His shirt was light blue and way too small for a man his size.

"Err, hello?" I muttered.

Cecilia held back a giggle behind me. She was clearly nervous. I turned and glared at her before looking at the man again.

We stared each other down for a few moments in a game of chicken. Who was going to speak first? I lost.

"Hello?" I asked confused. Why would he show up at the basement door of this place and not speak? It was intimidating.

"Who are you?" he demanded.

He had a booming voice, as if he was speaking through a megaphone. It was thick with an accent that I didn't recognize.

I felt like this conversation was completely reversed. Shouldn't I be the one asking the question? He had already taken control.

"Um, I'm Ryan," I stuttered. "Who

are you?" I asked.

He scoffed. "Name's Jason. Are there other people besides you two housed down there?"

He peered over my shoulder. I looked behind me and saw Cecilia standing there with her arms crossed. Confusion was plastered on her face.

"No. It's just my girlfriend and me," I stated. "Why?"

In hindsight, I should have lied.

He scowled. "Have you considered the fact that the world has completely fallen to pieces around you? It's the damn apocalypse!"

I remembered the city below us—a city that was completely devastated. The skyline was hazy. The crumbling buildings were surreal. The view from the shelter's gate was like a scene in those crazy sci-fi movies that seem overly edited—too much CGI.

I shuddered at the word. Apocalypse. The end of the world as we knew it. It had been talked about for ages. Feared by mankind for centuries. Nobody believed it was coming.

But if this was truly the apocalypse, then the disasters weren't over. This was just the beginning. I shook the thought from my mind and focused on the man in front of me. What was I supposed to do about him?

"Yes, sir, we're very well aware," I replied slowly, still feeling uncertain about his intentions.

Jason looked at me again and peered over my shoulder and down the stairs.

"How long did you plan on keeping this shelter a secret, kiddo?" he demanded.

Cecilia took in a deep breath and released her grip on my arm.

"Excuse me?" I asked sharply. "It isn't a secret."

The man rolled his eyes. I began to feel that he was dangerous. I had no idea how we were going to get rid of him, especially since he knew we were staying here.

"Well, kid, this shelter looks like it's in pretty good shape. Better than anything topside. Obviously you two have made yourselves at home here. When were you going to let other survivors know that this place was functioning?"

I thought my answer through. It did seem pretty selfish of us to not seek out other survivors who might want to join us here. I'd been so focused on making sure Cecilia was safe that I hadn't begun to consider the fact that other people needed help too. My bad.

"Well, we just got settled in here the other day. We planned on going out in search of other people who needed help today," I lied.

He grunted. "Like I'm really supposed to believe that?"

I was starting to get angry. This man thought he could show up here and start bossing us around. No way. No how.

"Well, sir, believe whatever you'd like. Thank you for checking up on us.

We'll see you around," I said.

I knew that he would challenge me. But I wanted him to know that I was in charge. I started to shut the doors on him. Just as they were about to close, he jammed his foot between the heavy doors.

"Son, I don't think you understand what I'm saying," Jason responded.

There was now a dangerous tone in his voice. I realized that we'd probably end up having to do things his way, especially since he was so big.

I tried to decide how to get him to go away without pissing him off even more and putting our safety at risk.

"Sir, I believe that right now it's every man for himself, and I'm worried about our safety," I said forcefully.

Jason removed his foot from the doorway and growled, "Selfish punks! There are dying women and babies out there! You two kids aren't the only people who were caught up in this catastrophe!"

I admit that he made some good points. There was enough room in the shelter for at least twenty more people. It was the food supply that I was worried about. If we allowed that many people to come into the shelter, our five-week maximum would go down to two or maybe even less. I wasn't prepared to put ourselves in that kind of danger. But then again, if more people were willing to help, we could find more resources even quicker. These were decisions that were out of my league. Cecilia tugged on my sleeve.

"Ryan," she whispered. "He's right. We aren't being fair. We don't own this property."

I wanted to scream that this wasn't about being fair! This was about life and death! But if we wanted to live, we'd have to be fair because we couldn't do this alone.

I turned back toward the man who was glaring at us with his huge brown eyes. I sighed.

"You're right. We can fit about twenty more people inside. Bring whoever you can find that looks healthy and safe. Especially kids. Cecilia can put together a plan for the food, and I'll prep the rooms."

Jason nodded. "That sounds more like it. Thank you for setting this boy's mind straight, Cecilia. Is there anything warmer down there that I can wear?"

Without a word, Cecilia raced downstairs. Jason and I continued our stare down.

When she reappeared, she handed Jason a big parka that we'd noticed earlier.

"I'll be back," Jason muttered.

I hoped he wouldn't.

Cecilia only nodded. I shut the door. That guy was really going to get on my nerves, I could tell.

"Well," I started. "Let's go get this place ready I guess."

Day 13

11:00 a.m.

Cecilia took a deep breath as if to say something. Then the coughing began. It started out soft at first, but then accelerated quickly into what almost sounded like an asthma attack. I ran over and grabbed her as she started to keel over from the severity of it.

When it finally eased, she looked extremely ill. Sweat dotted her face, and her eyes were bright red. She felt really hot. I picked her up and carried her downstairs into her bedroom. I laid her on the bed where she stayed for a few minutes with her eyes closed, taking deep breaths.

"Cecilia?" I asked worriedly, putting my hand on her forehead. She held up her finger, as if to tell me to hold on, and took a few more deep breaths. After a few moments she sighed and opened her eyes, which quickly filled with tears.

"What happened?" I asked. I was so confused.

"Ryan, something is wrong," she whispered.

"What do you mean?" I placed my hand on hers, and she held it tightly.

"I mean, I think I'm sick. Really sick. It started last night," she confessed.

"Why didn't you wake me up?" I demanded. She knew I would have gotten up to help her.

"Well, two reasons. One, I didn't want to scare you. And two, I couldn't make it to your room. I had this horrible nightmare; vivid colors and scary stuff that I can't really remember," she said. "I woke up sweating and feeling really sick to my stomach. I got up to walk to the bathroom. And I had a coughing fit kind of like what just happened. I'm surprised you didn't hear me." She continued, "Then I threw up. It finally all passed, and I tried to go back to sleep. But I couldn't. So I was awake all night. Then decided I would get up to make you breakfast. That's why I've been in such a bad mood. I'm so tired, and …

and I didn't want to scare you."

Tears were rolling down her face now.

I felt so helpless.

My heart broke. I think out of all the pain in the world, the feeling of your heart breaking has to be one of the worst. Not now. Not after losing everything. I looked at Cecilia and realized that she was my future. If I lost her now, I'd be nothing. I'd have no one. I hated how I'd been so cold to her earlier. It was all behind me now. All I wanted to focus on was getting her better.

"Ryan, say something. You've been staring blankly at me for like two minutes." She laughed and wiped a tear away from under her eye.

"We have to get you into bed. I need to look for medicine. There has to be some stored around here somewhere." I was rambling on and on under my breath. She didn't understand how determined I was to get her better. There was nothing I hated more than seeing her have to suffer.

"No. Ryan, stop. We have to get the shelter ready for the other people coming in!"

I stopped mumbling and sharply turned to look at her. "There's no way we're having other people join us. Maybe Jason won't make it back. We need everything here to keep you better. We can barricade the entrance."

Cecilia frowned. "That doesn't sound very fair. We can worry about me later, Ryan. There are people who need a place to stay. I promised Jason. Plus it's the right thing to do."

I softened up. Cecilia was able to put away her problems to make sure everyone else's were solved. She was never selfish. That was one of the things that attracted me to her in the first place.

"All right. But tonight I'm focused on getting you well. And you probably shouldn't be in too much contact with the other people coming in. We don't need any more sick people."

She nodded. "I know. I think I'll just keep my distance. But I want to be here to greet them. And to make sure Jason doesn't tear your head off!"

I laughed. There probably was a little truth to that lame joke.

"Are you going to work on getting some food together or would you rather rest?" I asked as she was standing up.

"Yes," she replied, dusting her hands on her pants. "I'll just be careful preparing the food. There are gloves in the kitchen. And I'll use a bandana to cover my mouth. Why don't you make sure the extra bedrooms are set up and stocked? Oh, and try to figure out how many people can fit in each room."

I nodded, agreeing. Cecilia would be much better off setting up the food. She stood up and wobbled for a few seconds. I put my hand on her elbows, steadying her.

"Are you okay?" I asked worriedly.

"Yes," she muttered. I knew she wasn't telling the truth, but I decided not to push it.

"Okay, well, will you be all right in the kitchen for a while? I'll just be down the hall. If you need *anything* holler, okay?"

"Okay, babe," she said smiling.

I walked over to her and placed a kiss on her forehead. I was so happy that she was with me. We were so lucky to have been together when the earthquake struck. Without each other, we would have been nothing.

Day 13

Noon

We both left the bedroom and headed out in opposite directions. I went into the bedroom next door to mine. Instead of one full-size bed, it had two small cots with thick mattresses and two pillows each. I decided that the minimum guests would be two. But we could definitely figure out a way to fit four. The bathroom was similar to mine, but it had a tub-shower combo. I figured that this room would probably be suitable for kids, since the young ones would probably prefer taking a bath.

The bedroom next door to that one had the biggest bed. The bathroom was the same as the one with the two cots, and I decided that probably a mom and her kids would enjoy this room.

It hit me that we may soon be dealing with children who were now orphans. It was going to kill Cecilia to see those kids. I remembered how she reacted with the little boy we'd passed days ago. I sort of wished now that we'd taken him along with us. Although there were no promises that he would have made it. It would've been harder to see him dying than to just let him go like we did. I tried to convince myself that that was true. Maybe if we were lucky, Jason would find him and bring him here. The chances were slim, but there was always hope. I felt like a bastard now for leaving him.

The rest of the bedrooms were just different versions of the ones I'd already seen. The maximum number of people we could shelter would be twenty. It'd be cramped. And it would mean Cecilia and I would have to share a room, but it was definitely doable. I just prayed we'd have enough food until we found other sources.

Day 13

5:00 p.m.

A long while later we heard the same familiar heavy knocking at the entrance to the basement. Jason had made it back.

By this time Cecilia had managed to piece together enough snacks to feed the survivors. I'd managed to figure out a couple ways to divide the bedrooms. Before going to answer the door, I walked up to Cecilia and gave her a hug and kiss.

"You know you're amazing?" I whispered, placing a kiss on her lips.

She blushed. I could never get over how beautiful she was.

"Go get the door. Be nice. But be firm. Jason seems like he could be really nice. He is rescuing people. We didn't. That says a lot. I'll remember to not get too close to any of the people," Cecilia said.

"All right, baby, I got this." Although of course, I really didn't.

I climbed the stairs for the second time that day. I slowly walked toward the large doors. I took a deep breath and detached the deadbolt. And I opened one of the doors. But I wasn't really ready to face whatever came next.

When I opened the door, Jason stood there with the same smirk he'd greeted us with earlier. The second he realized it was me, the grin turned into a scowl. Behind him were five people. Only about a quarter of what I was expecting. Was this it?

One of them was a tall lady who was much too slim to be healthy. She had long black hair and bright green eyes. She looked in about the same state Cecilia and I were in a few days ago.

Standing next to her was younger girl who looked like an eighth-grader. I guessed that she was the lady's daughter because she was almost the spitting image of the woman. She had medium-length black hair and ivory skin. Her eyes were brown and filled with anticipation and sadness. She also looked super skinny.

Standing behind the two was a little boy who looked really young. Six? Seven? He had dirty-blond hair and bright blue eyes. In his hand he held a ragged piece of cloth, which looked like what once was a blanket. He was wearing a ripped pair of khaki shorts and a Superman T-shirt that had one sleeve missing. Luckily he had on boots and a heavy coat. His cheeks were bright red. From his eyes and gestures you could tell that he was shy. I couldn't believe he'd made it. It was freakin' cold out there.

Next to him stood a man. He was tall, lanky, and really nerdy. He had on a pair of glasses that were crooked and nearly hung off one side of his face. His beard was scraggly and dirty. His eyes were small and beady—too small to determine the actual color. I pegged him as a brainy type. I hoped he would be handy.

Finally, standing beside him was a dude who looked just about my age. He was built and muscular in a healthy looking sort of way. His hair was long and jet black. He had to continually flip it, so it wouldn't get in his eyes— a habit that bugged me. Pet peeve, actually. Dude, get a haircut. And how come you have a tan in the dead of winter? And from the shape his clothes were in, it didn't look like he'd been through the end of the world at all.

He looked more like he had just gotten out of gym class. A little frazzled and a little dirty, but all in all, fine.

After a few seconds of silence, Jason coughed and took a breath, preparing to introduce me.

"Well, kid, these are the only people that I could rally up who were nearby. I'm sure there's more on the other side of town, but you and I can go and search there tomorrow."

He pointed to the two females and began the introductions.

"This right here is Renee and her daughter, Brittany. Luckily, they were able to stick together through all of this hell," Jason intoned.

I reached my hand out and shook Renee's hand and nodded at Brittany who blushed and looked down at the ground. "Name's Ryan," I said with emphasis. I stared squarely at Jason.

"And this young soldier right here is Daniel. He's been wandering the streets for days, trying to find someone to help him. Luckily, I grabbed him on our way back here!"

I smiled in sympathy toward the little boy and knelt down to greet him.

"Hey, Daniel, glad you could join us!" I held my hand out and the boy smiled and shook it weakly.

I stood up and was introduced to the tall, awkward man who was named Henry. He greeted me with a high-pitched voice, almost as awkward as his body.

Then I met Michael, whose voice

was deep and quiet. I could tell he probably wasn't someone to mess with. I wondered what Cecilia would think of him.

"Well, you guys can follow me down, and I'll give you a tour," I said. "You've already seen the trashed ground floor."

They all followed me in single file as if they were about to embark on a museum tour. I led them past the living area and toward the kitchen where I was expecting to find Cecilia. In the kitchen there were snacks all perfectly arranged. But Cecilia was nowhere to be seen. I heard a few gasps as our new housemates saw the food. And I decided right then that this was definitely the right thing to do.

"Please help yourselves, and make yourselves feel—for lack of a better word—at home. I'm going to go try to find my girlfriend, Cecilia. She should be around here somewhere," I said.

I wasn't sure who heard me because they were all devouring the food.

"Thank you so much for letting us stay here," Renee said, tears filling her eyes. "We weren't going to last much longer."

"Don't worry about it," I replied, remembering the feeling of such relief when we'd arrived here. "We were just lucky to find this place."

Day 13

6:00 p.m.

I started my search for Cecilia. I first looked in some of the bedrooms to see if she was checking my set-up skills. When she wasn't in there, I checked her room. I found her lying on her bed in the same position she'd been lying in earlier when she got sick. My stomach dropped to my feet. I couldn't deal with seeing her so sick.

"Babe?" I asked running over to her side.

She sighed. "I'm fine. Sorry. I was just sorting food, and I felt really dizzy, so I came to lie down before it got worse."

I put my hand on her head. It wasn't as hot as it'd been earlier, but it was still warmer than usual.

"We have to find some medicine for you, Cecilia. Before this gets worse."

I was terrified. It had never crossed my mind that sickness was going to be an issue. I mean obviously, eventually it would be. Illness wasn't something you could avoid. Even if you're lucky enough to survive the biggest building crashing down on you as the world collapses, the tiniest germs still have a way of sticking it to you.

But did the shelter even have medicine other than a simple first aid kit?

If not, where was I supposed to get some?

"Ryan, I don't really know if this is something medicine can fix," she whispered.

Dang! She really knew how to terrify a guy.

"What are you talking about? Of course it would!" I cried out. I was about to break. I couldn't stand and watch her be so sick and not be able to do anything about it. It was too much for me to handle.

She opened her eyes. They were red and glassy.

"Ryan, don't worry. I think we should give it a couple days before we get too afraid of anything. I'm not scared yet. I just feel really gross. I think my body is processing everything that's happened," she said. "I think this might be grief."

"I can't make that better. I try not to think about it. Well, um, do you feel good enough to come say hi? Would you rather me just tell them you're sleeping?" I asked.

She sighed. "I want to go meet everyone. How many are there? Is there enough food?"

"There are only five people, not including Jason. And there's plenty of food," I said.

Her eyes widened in surprise. "Five? I thought Jason was expecting twenty."

I shrugged my shoulders. I didn't know, but I wasn't complaining. At least we'd have enough food and stuff to last us long enough to figure something else out.

"Well, what kind of people are they?" she asked. "Nobody too sketchy, right?"

"You mean except for Jason?" I asked.

"Ryan, be serious," Cecilia nagged.

"There's a mom and a daughter ... The kid seems pretty young. Middle school? She's hilarious. She has the funniest lisp. And then there's this guy named Henry, who's real nerdy. But he seems like a nice guy. I hope he's smart," I continued. "And then there's this little boy who looks like that boy we ditched. It kills me to look at him. I feel so bad ..." Cecilia touched my arm.

57

"Anyway," I went on, "he's real cute. You'll love him. His name is Daniel. There's also this guy named Michael. Looks like he's eighteen or so. Buff. So no, nobody too sketchy … except Jason," I said again. I was only half kidding.

She smiled. "I want to meet the little boy. I'm feeling better. If I start feeling sick again, I'll come in here or signal you or something."

She sat up, took a deep breath, and swung her legs over the side of the bed.

"I'm going to wash my face and stuff. Then I'll be out there," Cecilia stated.

I nodded and gave her a kiss on her cheek before she went into the bathroom.

I made my way back into the kitchen where people were getting more acquainted with one another. Henry and Renee were chatting. Brittany helped Daniel clean up the mess of crumbs he'd made. Michael was sitting quietly listening to Jason ramble on about something that I'm sure had no importance.

Jason saw me and smirked. "Where's Cecilia at, kid?"

"Dude, my name's Ryan," I snapped. He was really irritating. I held back any other wise remarks. I replied, "She's coming. She's washing her face. She was napping."

Just as I finished explaining, Cecilia came in behind me. She was wearing a pair of gray sweats we'd found in an empty room. Her hair was hanging loosely and her cheeks were rosy— probably from the fever. She still managed to look breathtaking. How did she do that?

Everyone stopped talking and stared at her. She awkwardly waved. Then she nervously giggled.

"Hey, I'm Cecilia. Sorry, I fell asleep."

Henry was the first one to get up to greet her. He offered out his hand to shake, but Cecilia politely shook her head.

"I don't want to get any of you guys sick. I've been feeling a bit under the weather. But it's really nice to meet you."

Obviously nobody was thinking about the loss of modern medicine and what they could possibly catch from Cecilia because one by one, everyone greeted her.

Henry smiled. "I'm Henry. Nice to meet you. Thank you for prepping all of this food. It means a lot."

Cecilia smiled in return. "You're so welcome. I'm so glad all of you guys are okay."

Renee stood up next and introduced herself. "Hey, sweetheart. I'm Renee, and that's my daughter, Brittany."

Brittany then stood up and walked next to her mom and offered Cecilia a smile full of braces.

Daniel stayed sitting in his chair, but looked up timidly at Cecilia. I knew immediately that she would fall in love with Daniel. She loved little kids.

"And you must be Daniel," Cecilia said tenderly.

Daniel nodded and smiled at Cecilia.

Day 13

7:00 p.m.

After everyone chatted for a while, I realized that Jason had disappeared. I thought this was strange. He hadn't told me he was leaving the shelter. I needed to lay down the law that technically, Cecilia and I had control over this place. We found it first. That was going to be a hard thing to convince him of because he was huge. He was the only person that sort of set me off. I know he liked Cecilia, and Cecilia didn't seem to have a problem with him. But I felt like something wasn't right about him. It was more than the fact that he tried everything he could do to piss me off.

I walked over to where Cecilia and Henry were talking and tapped her on the shoulder.

"Cecilia, where'd Jason go?" I asked.

She scanned the room. "He didn't tell me he was going anywhere. I have no clue."

Suspicion arose inside me. Where would he have gone? He didn't know where the bathrooms were. No one had claimed a room yet. It was odd and unsettling to picture him walking around the shelter. I didn't know why.

I decided to check things out, so I

left the kitchen and walked down the hallway. I had left all of the bedroom doors open after I prepped them. It threw me off that they were all now closed. What the ...?

"Jason?" I called out. I was really steamed. I couldn't decide whether I was more creeped out or pissed off that he'd obviously been going through the rooms. It wasn't like there was anything he could steal. It was the fact that he was being sneaky.

When I got no reply, I decided to investigate further. I opened the first bedroom door. Nothing changed. No Jason. The next three rooms were the same as the first. Nothing changed. No Jason. I then approached the two bedrooms at the end of the hall, which were Cecilia's and mine. It would be just plain weird to find him in my bedroom, but it'd be downright creepy to find him in Cecilia's. The guy looked like he was at least thirty. Was he interested in Cecilia? Weird! Gross!

If we were in danger, there was absolutely no government agency that could help us. We were on our own. It sounded like a sci-fi horror movie. Survivors of the end of the world are all stuck together. One by one they begin disappearing. Nobody can decide who the killer is until there's only two left. And then—I shook the thoughts out of my head. I needed to be levelheaded and not jump to any conclusions.

I walked up to my room and opened it just a crack. Nothing. The bed was still the same. Jason was nowhere to be seen. I gulped. That either meant he was wandering around somewhere else in the shelter or he was in Cecilia's room.

I shut my bedroom door and walked directly to the bedroom across from mine. I had some strange feeling that Jason really was in there. I took a few deep breaths. This guy had me rattled. What was it about him that creeped me out so much? I knocked on the door. No reply. I knocked a few more times and finally got a muffled "humph" in reply. A few seconds later the door opened and there stood Jason, zipping up his fly.

"What are you doing in here?" I demanded.

He laughed. "Is a man not allowed to use the john around here?"

"Why did you use Cecilia's bathroom? Why didn't you ask? Why did you have to go into every other bedroom first? Dude, what's *wrong* with you?" I asked.

I threw questions at him, one after another. They didn't seem to faze him like I thought they would.

"First of all, I was checking out the bedrooms. By the time I was done, I had to take a leak. So I decided you wouldn't mind if I relieved myself. I didn't even know this was your girl's room."

Jason lowered himself down to my level and put his face close to mine. His breath reeked and almost made me gag. He said, "Don't question me, kid. I'm definitely not the type of guy you want to mess with."

After saying those words, he raised his shoulders back up and brushed past me, leaving me in the doorway of Cecilia's bedroom. I was right. This guy definitely wasn't safe enough to have in the shelter without protection. I decided that I needed to discuss things with Cecilia. Together we could decide whether or not to kick him out. At a minimum we could warn Henry and Michael about him, so they could help me out if he did become a threat.

After I'd calmed down a little bit, I walked back into the kitchen. Everyone had opened up. There was laughter and conversation. Cecilia was seated next to Jason and Henry. The three of them were deep in conversation. When I walked in, Jason glanced up at me. With his eyes, he signaled me to keep my mouth shut. This guy was really beginning to worry me.

I decided to go ahead and let everyone know the rooms were ready. Everyone could get settled in, and I could talk to Cecilia. I cleared my throat and began to signal for everyone's attention.

"I just want to let you all know that the bedrooms are ready," I said. "And I'd be happy to help you all settle in."

"There are actual bedrooms?" Brittany asked full of hope.

I smiled at her, "There sure are. And showers! With hot water. I'm sure you're all anxious to get cleaned up."

Everyone in the room chuckled and murmured in agreement. It had been a brutal two weeks for all of us.

They all stood up and followed me back into the hallway where I was ready with room assignments.

Day 13

8:00 p.m.

It made sense that Michael and little Daniel would have the room with the two cots. They both took off to clean up. Henry had one of the single rooms. So did Jason. But I made sure Jason had the room farthest down from Cecilia. Finally, it was decided that Brittany and Renee would share my big bed, and I'd move into Cecilia's room with her. I mostly made that work just so I could make sure Cecilia was safe from Jason.

After making sure everyone was settled in, Cecilia and I retreated to our room. She yawned and threw herself down on the bed.

"I'm exhausted!" she exclaimed.

"How are you feeling?" I asked anxiously. I really hoped that whatever she had wasn't long term. Maybe it *was* just grief. I didn't want to worry her about Jason, but I had to ask her what she thought.

"Honestly, I feel better. I'm still sort of queasy and really tired."

She smiled at me from the bed. She did look like she was feeling better. I decided to tell her about Jason the creep.

"Cecilia, there's something off about Jason," I stated. She looked at me with confusion.

"What do you mean, Ryan? He seems really nice. He saved all these people. I know you guys got off to a rough start, but I think everything is fine," she said.

Darn it. He'd already convinced her to be on his side.

"I know. That was heroic of him. But, Cecilia, I found him in your room earlier. *This* room."

She looked at me strangely. "Doing what?" she asked.

"I don't honestly know. When he disappeared earlier, I came to see where he'd gone. I don't really know what he was doing in here, but he said he was using the restroom."

"In *my* bathroom? Ew. Why?" She seems truly grossed out.

I shrugged my shoulders. "I have no idea. But that's why I'm saying that something isn't right."

She looked at me worriedly. "You really think he's a threat?"

I didn't want to scare her. But I honestly did feel threatened. And I'm a big guy. But he was intimidating. I wanted him out. But he had just saved five people. I wasn't going to make any alliances. What was I supposed to do?

"I really do," I replied. I walked over and sat down on the bed next to her. "I mean, I don't have any proof to think that he is, except what I told you. There's this feeling deep in my gut that there's really something wrong with the guy."

"Your gut has always been right, Ryan. I'm scared." Cecilia took my hand and squeezed it hard.

"I know you are. I am too. But I think we should just keep an eye on him and see what he does for the next couple of days. Then we can decide what to do from there," I suggested.

Just then there was a knock on our door. Cecilia gasped. My blood began pumping. What if Jason had heard us talking? I scanned the room looking for some sort of weapon to use if I needed one. There wasn't anything except a lamp.

"Ryan, what do we do?" Cecilia whispered.

I tried giving her a reassuring look and slowly walked toward the door. I approached the door and turned the knob, mentally preparing myself for whatever could be behind it. What a relief to see Renee standing there!

"Hey, kids, sorry to bother you guys!" she greeted us cheerfully.

Cecilia laughed. "Your not bothering us, trust me."

I smiled at Renee and asked her to come in.

"Oh no, thank you. I'm about to go to sleep, but I just wanted to thank you guys again for having us stay here. It's such a blessing. I don't know what I would have done if I'd lost Brittany. We were cutting it close, and only God could've helped this all work out."

I smiled. I knew exactly how she felt. "Renee, you're welcome. We're thankful that Jason found you guys in time."

Renee furrowed her brow. "Now," she leaned in closer. "Does something seem not right to you about that Jason guy?"

I was surprised and relieved that I wasn't the only one who thought that Jason wasn't exactly the sanest looking guy.

"We think so too. That's actually what we were just talking about. We're trying to figure out what to do," I confided.

Renee nodded thoughtfully. "Well, I'm keeping my eye on him. He kept giving Brittany strange looks. And I don't think I like him very much. He did lead us here, but … Keep me updated, okay? Sleep well, kids, see you in the morning."

I nodded and smiled back. "Will do. See you the morning."

After that, she walked back down the hallway, and I shut the door.

Cecilia washed her face in the bathroom, came back out, and crawled into bed. I washed up and wondered how to prepare for the worst. Then I walked back into the bedroom and crawled into the bed next to Cecilia. She wrapped her arms around me and kissed me on the cheek.

"You're the best, baby! You know that?" she whispered.

I turned and looked her in the eyes. She was so pretty.

"I don't know that, but it's always

nice to hear you say it. Good night, my love," I whispered back and kissed her softly on the lips.

I'd promised our moms that I would be a perfect gentleman, and I was sticking to that promise.

Day 13

9:00 p.m.

I turned off the light. Just as I began to drift off, I was jerked awake by a bloodcurdling scream.

Cecilia jumped up and looked at me. We both struggled to comprehend what was happening. Who was screaming and why?

My mind raced, and I began to prepare myself for the worst. What had we gotten ourselves into and what were we going to do? I scrambled out of bed and rushed to the door. I grabbed the lamp. I could have used it as a weapon. But honestly, I was completely unprepared to face whatever horror might be waiting on the other side of that door.

About the Author

Sara Michelle

As a high school student, I never thought that I could pursue my creative interests. But with the support of my family, I auditioned to attend an arts magnet program in south-central Texas. I'm so excited to be going to a school that lets me explore my right brain and harnesses my imagination.

Speaking of interests ... those would involve: singing, songwriting, dancing, reading, going out with friends, spending money, and—writing. I love this time in my life and plan to live it up while doing what I used to believe was impossible, writing and publishing books. One day I'd love to get my PhD in psychology—and in a parallel universe, I'd love to be an actor. My favorite food is ice cream; I could honestly live off of it 24/7. My friends mean the world to me, and I'd be absolutely nowhere without my large, crazy family. I can't wait to see what life has to offer, and I plan on enjoying every minute of it!

My New Normal™

The following is an excerpt from

The Others, Book 3...

Day 14

9:55 a.m.

When I was in fourth grade, I was tormented by the class bully, Jeffery Hugh. He was a husky kid with bright orange hair and freckles everywhere. He always told me that I was stupid or fat. But what hurt me the most was when he told me that when the world ended, I was going to be the only one left behind. I never thought that he would be right.

My thoughts drifted back to the events of last night. I remember Renee coming in to wish us a good night's sleep. And I remember snuggling with Ryan and getting ready to fall asleep. Then we heard the scream. I was completely terrified. We were defenseless.

When we opened the door, the screaming continued. Ryan grabbed the lamp. I was honestly terrified. I knew Ryan was too because when I grabbed his hand, it was shaking. If you think rationally, it was ridiculous for teenagers to deal with this kind of threat. We'd already witnessed the world falling to pieces. We'd lost everyone and everything we loved. We'd both been dreadfully ill. Who knew what was going to hit us next?

We followed the scream, and it led us into the living area with the two couches and broken TV. We peeked around the corner and what we saw made my stomach seize. Renee was facing Jason. She was talking madly and gesturing wildly. I didn't realize why until I saw what Jason was holding in his hand. One of the butcher knives from the kitchen was firmly in his right hand. His face looked smug, slightly annoyed, and almost threatening. Renee continued her ranting.

...For more, get your copy of The Others, Book 3 today!